Co

written by John Lockyer
illustrated by Kelvin Hawley

The Magrister, a small trainer jet, climbed high into the sky. From the rear seat, Adam picked out the patchwork of yellow desert sands below. It looked so distant. He glanced at the altimeter – they had reached maximum height.

Now for the fun!

Adam's helmet receiver crackled. "Ready?" asked his father. "Ready," said Adam, gripping his seat. There would be barrels, loops, Cuban eights and (hopefully) a new move that would thrill him with fear. His father laughed. "Here we go! Down! Down! Down!"

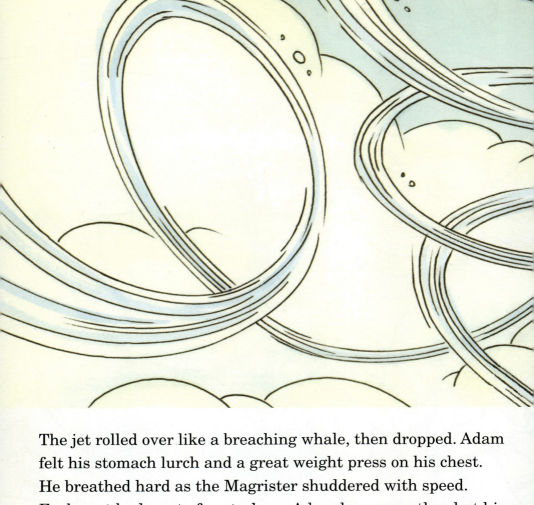

The jet rolled over like a breaching whale, then dropped. Adam
felt his stomach lurch and a great weight press on his chest.
He breathed hard as the Magrister shuddered with speed.
Each seat had a set of controls, so Adam knew exactly what his
father – a test pilot – was doing. With the booster pedals jammed
against the floor and the hand column thrust forward, the jet
was in a vertical dive. When the column came back and the nose
rose up, Adam had to close his eyes because everything went
topsy-turvy as they swung through wild rolls, loops and spirals.
Then the Magrister evened out and everything became smooth.

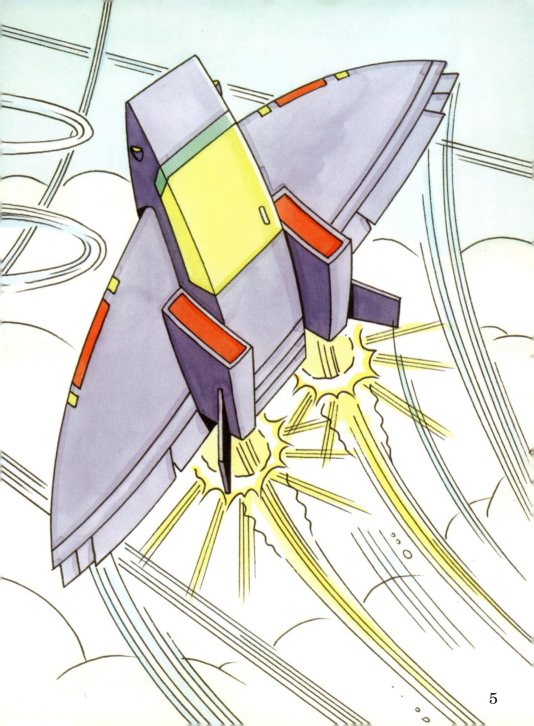

"Here it comes," thought Adam. "The new move."

But nothing happened. He opened his eyes. The pedals and column were still. He looked at his father and saw his head slumped forward.

"Dad?" he said.

Silence.

"Dad!"

Then he remembered that during the pre-flight check his father had kept shaking his head. When Adam asked him what was wrong, he said, "Just an annoying headache."

Had his dad blacked out?

Adam felt fear flutter within him. He looked out of the cockpit. Far in the distance was the inky-black homing strip. He let out a burst of breath. At least they were still on course. But…what if… his father didn't come around? Would he… could he fly the jet? Adam had taken the controls before, but only with his Dad guiding him through turns, climbs and descents. That had been fun. This wasn't!

He stared at his father's head. "Wake up, Dad… Please!"

As the jet started shaking and wobbling, Adam looked at the instrument panel and groaned. He hit the yellow pad below the communicator light. It should have been his first action. His helmet filled with static then quietened. "Hello Tower!" he said. "This is… Adam… Pilot Heming's son… Something's wrong with my Dad. He can't fly!"

He released the pad. His helmet filled with static again, then he heard faraway voices.

"Hello," he said. The voices weakened. He twisted a knob and they faded out altogether. He glanced out of the cockpit. The jet had dropped below the mountain tops and was swinging away from the homing strip. He felt fear grip him again. They were off course!

Suddenly rough air threw the jet sideways. Without thinking, Adam grabbed the column with one hand and hit a large red pad with the other hand. "Code Red! Code Red!" he shouted. It was the call sign for a crash landing. If the tower got the message then emergency teams would be on full alert. It was at that moment that he became aware he had the column in his hand. He was flying the jet.

Alone!

In his mind, Adam saw the controls being worked by his father as he had many times before and felt a tiny sliver of sureness. "Gently, gently," he muttered, easing the column back. "Get back on course."

The speed dropped, but Adam kept his eyes on a panel dial that
flickered red. When it turned green – a safe speed for landing –
he shifted the column forward. Next he tapped a booster pedal
with his foot. He kept tapping it until another dial shone green.
The Magrister was back on course. If the speed or direction
changed, tracking beams from the homing strip would flick the
dials back into red.

All Adam had to do now was to keep the jet steady. He should
have felt relieved, but he had a nagging doubt that there was
something else. Once more, he went over their other landings.
His Dad's actions went round and round inside his head.
Round and round.
And there it was.
What he had forgotten.
Wheels!

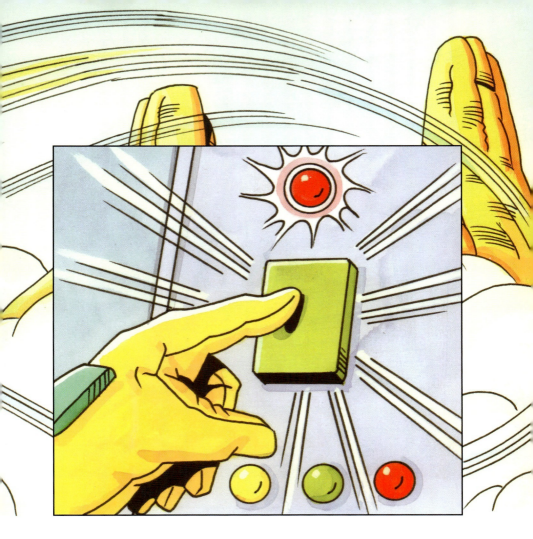

On the panel, another dial was flashing red. Thinking it was the landing gear alert, Adam hit the pad below it. There was a loud "whoosh" of blowing air. Every light on the panel flashed three times and disappeared. The engine whirred and died.

Silence.

He had hit the wrong pad. He had cut the power.

Adam felt his heart thump. The fear was back. But there was
nothing to do but hope. Hope that he had enough speed. Hope
that he kept the Magrister on course. Hope that the wheels were
down.

Outside, the desert rocks and dunes looked close enough to touch. The homing strip was under him. He eased the column back. The nose dropped. He pushed the column forward. The jet flattened out. It seemed to hang in the air then sank.

Adam waited for
the squeal of cold
rubber on hot tar, but
instead there was an
almighty thumping
crack, followed by the
shrieking of metal
ripping across the
blacktop. Smoke,
sparks and bits of
fuselage trailed
behind. Then the jet
twisted sideways,
came up onto one
wing, and seemed to
hang there as if it was
going to flip, before it
crashed back down and
sat still.

Immediately the cockpit popped open. Firm hands reached in, unclipped his harness and pulled him free. Drenched with sweat, coughing and spluttering, Adam was dragged clear of the wreck while firefighters sprayed the Magrister with foam.

But where was his Dad? Then he saw him. On a stretcher.
Adam ran to him.

"Is he okay?" he asked. The paramedic nodded. "He's unconscious,
but his signs are all good. Luckily he got you down to safety
before he passed out totally."

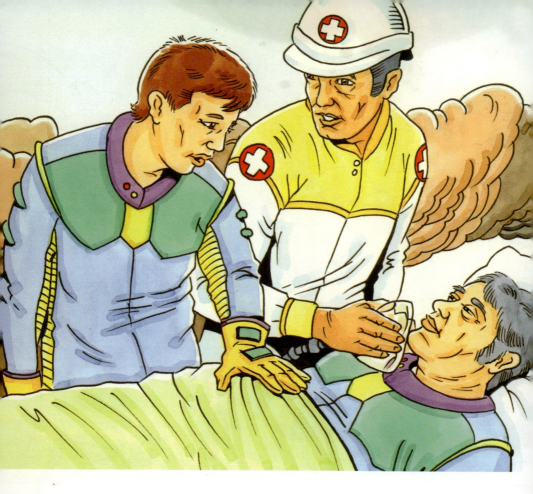

At that moment Adam's Dad opened his eyes and groaned. "It wasn't me," he said. "It was Adam. He landed the Magrister." Everyone stared at Adam. Their looks of disbelief slowly changed to understanding. Those few words explained the Code Red call and no landing gear.

Adam helped them lift his Dad into the ambulance. There wasn't time now, but soon he would have to tell his story: a story he hardly believed himself.